Let's Look at the Seasons

Autumn Days

By Ann Schweninger

VIKING

The art was prepared with graphite pencil,
colored pencil, and watercolor paint on Arches
90-pound cold-press watercolor paper.

VIKING
Published by the Penguin Group
Viking Penguin, a division of Penguin Books USA Inc.,
375 Hudson Street, New York, New York 10014, U.S.A.
Penguin Books Ltd, 27 Wrights Lane, London W8 5TZ, England
Penguin Books Australia Ltd, Ringwood, Victoria, Australia
Penguin Books Canada Ltd, 2801 John Street,
Markham, Ontario, Canada L3R 1B4
Penguin Books (N.Z.) Ltd, 182–190 Wairau Road,
Auckland 10, New Zealand

Penguin Books Ltd, Registered Offices:
Harmondsworth, Middlesex, England

First published in 1991 by Viking Penguin,
a division of Penguin Books USA Inc.

1   3   5   7   9   10   8   6   4   2

Library of Congress Catalog Card Number: 91-50199
ISBN 0-670-82758-4

Printed in U.S.A.   Set in ITC Cheltenham Light

For Dr. Isabel Wright

First Day

The first day of autumn is usually September 21st.

Autumn days are cool and short. The earth moves away from the warmth and light of the sun.

Early Autumn

Animals are getting ready
for winter.

A chipmunk carries seeds
in its cheek pouches. Then
it stores the seeds in
underground tunnels it
has dug.

Squirrels bury nuts to eat
later, when food is hard
to find.

Rabbits are eating lots of
leaves and grass. When
winter comes, they will eat
buds and bark.

A woodchuck eats leaves and
grass, too. When winter arrives, a
woodchuck is fat. It lives off the fat
as it sleeps through the winter.

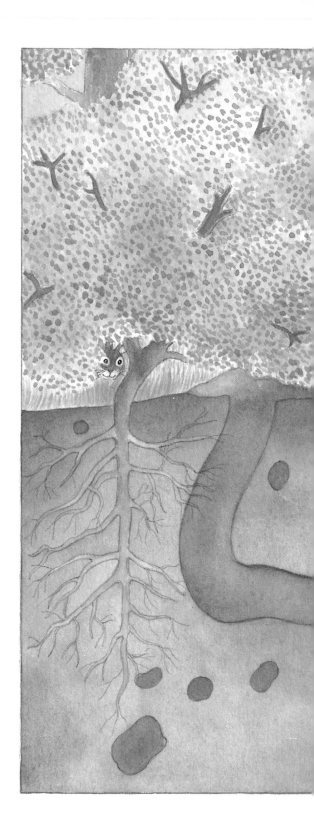

Harvest Time, Planting Time

In early autumn, many crops are ready to be harvested. You can pick apples, pumpkins, tomatoes, and squash.

For some crops, autumn is a time to plant. Rhubarb and radishes grow during cool autumn days. Winter wheat is planted now, too.

Did you plant a garden?

Autumn Plenty

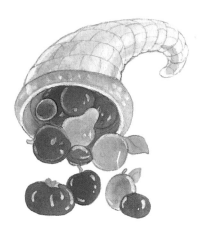

Fruits

Press apples to make
apple juice and cider.

Dry grapes
to make raisins.

Vegetables

Cut lettuce, radishes,
and scallions, then
toss a salad.

Grains

Grind and sift wheat to make flour.
Then bake flour into bread.

We use
grain
seeds.

wheat   rice   rye

Cook tomatoes
to make ketchup.

Slice peaches
for a peach pie.

Grate carrots
and bake a
carrot cake.

Slice and fry potatoes
to make French fries
and potato chips.

Boil corn to eat corn-on-the-cob.
Dry and pop corn to make popcorn.

Roll and cook oats
to make oatmeal.

barley   millet   corn   oats

October Fun

Insects in Autumn

Many insects die in cold weather. But first they lay eggs that will hatch in the spring.

A field cricket punches a hole in the ground with her egg placer. The eggs she lays will be safe underground until spring.

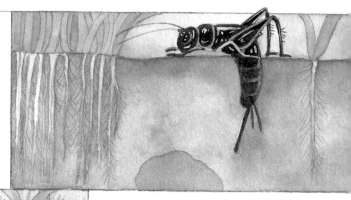

Ants do not die when cold weather comes. They stay underground in little tunnels they have made or in rotting wood. They eat food they stored during spring, summer, and autumn.

Honeybees gather nectar for making honey. They stay inside hollow trees or hives, and eat their honey all winter.

In autumn, monarch butterflies fly thousands of miles to spend the winter in warm places like Monterey, California, and northern Mexico.

Though days are cool, water striders still swim on the surfaces of ponds and streams. They will leave the water to spend the winter under fallen leaves near the water's edge.

Ladybugs have eaten many smaller bugs, such as aphids. Now a group of ladybugs crawls under leaves or bark to sleep all winter.

Adult firefly beetles, whose lights we see on summer nights, cannot live through cold weather. But their young, called glowworms, sleep underground until spring.

Banded woollybear caterpillars busily crawl here and there, searching for snug places to sleep during winter.

Legend says that if the woollybear caterpillar's reddish brown stripe is wide, winter will be cold. If it is narrow, winter will be mild.

Making a Leaf Wreath

Here's what you need:  lots of pretty leaves

a piece of heavy paper or thin cardboard

 a plate a small bowl

a pencil scissors

 glue masking tape  string

Outdoors, collect a lot of brightly colored leaves.

Indoors, set the plate on the piece of heavy paper or thin cardboard. Draw around the plate.

Put a small bowl in the center of the circle you have drawn, and draw around the bowl.

Cut around the outside circle.

Cut to the inside circle,
and around it. On the back
of the paper or cardboard,
tape closed the cut you
have made.

Glue as many leaves as
you want to the front.

Let the glue dry. Now tape
a 4-inch piece of string to
the back to make a hook.

Hang the wreath on a tack
or nail . . . and enjoy!

Indian Summer

In autumn, suddenly the days can become hot again, just like summer! This mild, dry, hazy time can last a few days or weeks.

In the days of the American colonies, the American Indians told colonists they could look forward to this pleasant time of year during autumn in America. And so colonists called it "Indian summer."

Autumn Tree

All summer, a tree grows. In autumn, it stops growing.

Even the roots have stopped growing.

A corky layer grows across the leaf stalk, here.

The leaf stops growing and changes color.

Green material in leaves is called chlorophyll. It takes sunlight and gases from the air, and water from the soil, and changes them into food for a tree.

During summer, we cannot see the gold, yellow, and orange colors that are in leaves because the green chlorophyll is a much brighter color. In autumn, there is less sunlight, so chlorophyll fades. Then we see the gold, yellow, and orange.

August

September

Autumn is also
called *fall*.

Some leaves turn bright red because food made by the
leaf has become trapped inside. The food turns bright
red, and so does the leaf.

On the ground, dead leaves provide food and cover for
insects. In the woods, mice hide under dead leaves. As
leaves decay, they nourish the soil and help other plants
to grow.

October

November

Halloween

First Frost

Autumn nights are chilly. When the temperature falls
below 32°, early morning dew freezes and becomes
frost. Frost looks like a thin layer of snow. It covers
plant leaves, and kills them.

When you go outside, you see
your breath in the cold air.

November

In late autumn, the earth moves farther and farther away from the sun. Each day is shorter than the one before. There is less sunlight, so days are cold.

Plants are not growing. It is harder for animals to find food. But grass seeds, berries, and acorns are ripe. There are still some apples on apple trees and grain can be found among the stubble of corn and wheat fields.

A Different Autumn

The widest part of the earth is called the equator. The sun shines more strongly there than anywhere on earth. The closer a place is to the equator, the warmer it is. Autumn is warm in Southern California and Texas because they are closer to the equator than Minnesota or New York, where autumn is cool.

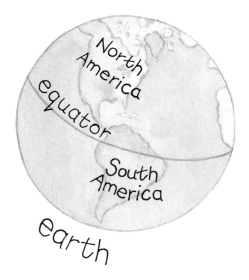

Thanksgiving

Now we celebrate Thanksgiving on the fourth Thursday in November. We give special thanks for all we have.

December

As autumn ends, birds eat seeds and dried berries. They fluff their feathers to stay warm.

A white-footed mouse nibbles seeds and nuts it has stored in its den inside an old log.

Fish swim slowly in cold water.

Underground, a toad is asleep until spring. It has dug down deep to keep out of the cold.

Animals with fur have grown thick coats.

When you go outside, bundle up!